OUTSIDE, INSIDE

LeUyen Pham

Andersen Press

First published in Great Britain in 2021 by Andersen Press Ltd.,
20 Vauxhall Bridge Road, London SW1V 2SA
Originally published in the USA in 2021 by Roaring Brook Press,
a division of Holtzbrinck Publishing Holdings Limited Partnership.
Published by special arrangement with Rights People, London.
Printed and bound in China.
10 9 8 7 6 5 4 3 2 1
British Library Cataloguing in Publication Data available.
ISBN 978 1 83913 117 2

Something strange
happened on an
unremarkable day
just before the season
changed.

Everybody who was

OUTSIDE....

. . . went .

Everyone.

Everywhere.

All
over
the
WORLD.

Everyone just went inside,
shut their doors,

and WAITED.

Well,
almost everyone.

Some people

NEEDED to be . . .

...where they
NEEDED to be.

THANK YOU ALL FOR SAVING MY WIFE'S LIFE

LOUNGE

OUTSIDE,
the sky was quiet,

but the wind still blew,

birds
kept
singing

and squirrels
played in
the streets,

but the cars stayed away.

The world felt
a little different.

INSIDE,

we baked and cooked,

made music and watched TV.

We read and played games.

Some of us worked a little,
some of us worked a lot ...

and some of us
couldn't work
at all.

We all felt
a little different.

OUTSIDE,
there were fences
both real
and pretend.

Swings sat still,
and slides
were lonely.

Bells didn't ring,
and halls
were empty.

We had birthdays
without parties,

shared words
without sounds,

and
reached
each other
without
touching.

The world was changing
a tiny bit outside.

INSIDE

we
laughed

and we worried,

and we cried,

and we tried to breathe.

We made things together

and did things alone.

We hoped and prayed and wished.

We were all changing a tiny bit inside.

OUTSIDE, the world kept growing.

INSIDE,
we kept growing too.

So why did we
all go inside?

Well . . .

...there were
lots of reasons.

But mostly
because
everyone
knew

it was the right
thing to do.

On the OUTSIDE,
we are all different.

But on the

we are all
the same.

And we remembered
that soon

spring would come.

INSIDE...

...and

OUTSIDE.

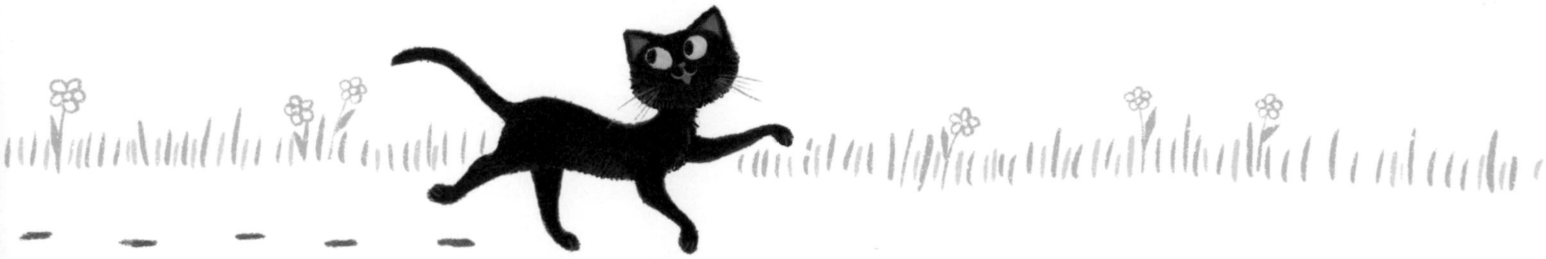